How Ella Grew an Electric Guitar

A Girl's First Adventure in Business

By Orly Sade
&
Ellen Neuborne

ISBN: 1-4611-4990-8
ISBN-13: 9781461149903

Dedication

We dedicate this book to our children

Mor and Tomer

Henry and Leslie

chapter

ONE

Have you ever wanted something really badly? Like a new bike or a cool jacket or the latest, greatest cell phone? Have you ever asked a grown-up and been told, "Money doesn't grow on trees"?

Me, too! Isn't that annoying? Believe me, I hear you.

This is the story of how I found out where money really does grow. So sit down, and I'll let you in on the secret. You'll have that new bike in no time!

It all started in the spring of sixth grade. Things were going pretty well for me. I was in the gifted and talented class at Susan B. Anthony Middle School in Greenwich Village (that's in Manhattan). My best friend, Madison, was also in my class and also had glasses, brown hair, and blue eyes, like me. I was getting good grades—especially in my favorite subject, which is math. And I was the lead singer in The Flash, the coolest, sweetest, most popular rock band in the whole sixth grade. Okay, we were the only rock band in the whole sixth grade. And we'd never played in public. Only in the basement of Madison's apartment building. But still, we knew we were destined for fame and fortune.

That spring, I really wanted two things:

A date with Tyler, our band drummer.

A new electric guitar.

I didn't know how to get either of the things I wanted. So I started with the guitar. That seemed less scary.

Every day, on our walk home from school, I made Madison detour past St. Mark's Place just so I could look in the window of Underground Sound at the Daisy Rock Stardust Elite electric guitar. It was a solid body, double cutaway. And best of all, it was purple, with glitter built right in so that it shined like jewelry. Every time I saw it, I knew it was the guitar for me. Then, I would see the price tag: $229.

One day after school, I dumped out the contents of my piggy bank: $25.

"Well, that's a start," said Madison, hopefully. She's the kind of person who always thinks everything's going to be okay.

"It's not much," I told her glumly. "And it's six months' worth of babysitting. Most of the good baby-sitting jobs go to older kids. I hardly ever get called. At this rate," I said, calculating in my head (which is my specialty), "I'll be in high school before I have the money."

"Wow," said Madison. "That's a long time."

"Yes," I agreed. "Too long. I need another plan."

That night at dinner, I waited until I'd eaten two helpings of chicken and all my broccoli before I brought up the idea to my parents. Dinner is a good time to talk to them. Unless one of them is on a business trip, we always eat dinner together, Mom, Dad, my brother Tom, and me. Generally, my parents are pretty cool. My dad is a lawyer. He says he's not the kind of lawyer you see on TV, but the kind of lawyer that helps businesses do more business. My mom designs computer software. She makes every machine in the house run. They are both constantly saying how important it is to get an education. So that's how I made my pitch.

"You know, I was thinking that I'd like to further my music education," I said as my bother Tom and I began to clear the table.

"Really? That sounds interesting," said Mom. "What did you have in mind?"

"A new electric guitar. I have it all picked out. It's a Daisy Rock Stardust electric. It's a solid body cutaway. It's purple and glittery and awesome, and it's for sale at Underground Sound for $229."

I saw Mom look at Dad over the table. That's never a good sign. I looked at Tom. He's fourteen. He mouthed the words "No way" as he gathered up the silverware and began to put it into the sink.

But I didn't give up that easily. "You always say music is educational," I said.

"Yes," said Dad. "That's why we bought you your first guitar. Why can't you play that one?"

"It's not electric," I told him.

"But it is musical," he said. "That's what counts."

"Not when you want to be a rock star," I answered.

"So much for education," muttered Tom from the sink. I glared at him, hoping he would shut up and stay out of it.

When I looked back at Mom and Dad, they had The Look.

If you are a kid, you know what The Look is. It's that way grown-ups look at you when you know you're not going to get your way, but first you have to listen to a lecture about it. Great, just great.

"This year, we have a lot of expenses," said Mom. "There's the rent and your brother's braces. And don't forget what happened to the car."

Who could forget that? The car—a blue station wagon older than my brother—had stopped running in the middle of the Long Island Expressway when we were on our way to summer vacation. We had to wait three hours in the burning hot sun for a tow truck. It was a nightmare. The only good thing to come of it was that they finally sold that old wreck and bought a new one. Mom said she was sad—the old car was like one of the family, she said. I sure didn't think so. Not that I thought the new car was so great. It didn't even have rear-seat TV screens. But apparently it was expensive.

"I don't think this is the year we can spend that kind of money on a new guitar, especially since your old one works just fine," said Dad. "After all, money doesn't grow on trees."

Oh, I hate that line.

I left the table and went to my room. I sat down at my computer and fired up my favorite search engine. I typed in the words "Where does money grow?"

I got 1,030,000,000 results.

I was thrilled. Surely, my answer was right here.

I clicked on the first result. It was a long document, with no pictures, about something called the Commerce Department. It didn't make much sense to me. There wasn't anything about getting money for an electric guitar.

I tried the second result.

"Your money deserves more!" This page had lots of pictures—of grown-ups smiling in front of big houses, cars, and boats. And they were all holding little plastic cards in their hands. Credit cards. I recognized those. I also knew kids didn't have them. So that wasn't going to work either.

Result number three: this was an article about finance. It looked interesting at first—all about bulls and bears. But soon it got confusing. It had so many words I didn't understand: stocks, bonds, mutual funds, annualized returns. Then there was all this stuff about bear markets. What did money have to do with bears?

I kept reading, page after page, but I was not getting any closer to my goal of finding out where money comes from.

"Ella, five minutes to bedtime," Mom called.

I knew finding the answer to my problem was going to take more than five minutes. I clicked off my computer. I would try again in the morning.

chapter

TWO

The next day, I went to school as usual. But time seemed to drag on and on and on. Even my favorite class felt like it was taking forever.

"What's with you?" asked Madison when I looked up from my math sheet for the millionth time to look at the clock on the wall.

"I've got things to do after school," I responded.

Madison raised her eyebrows in a "Huh?" gesture.

I continued. "I'm still not sure how I'm going to get money to buy the guitar. But I think I know who does have my answers. I just have to wait until school is over to ask the questions. Will this day ever end?"

Finally, the bell rang. I sprang from my seat. I was almost to the door when the teacher, Mr. Edwards, called to me.

"Ella, stay behind a moment, please," he said.

Madison gave me a sympathetic look as she walked out the door. I sighed and walked back into the room to face my teacher.

Mr. Edwards was very tall and had lots of curly hair. He smiled a lot, especially when his students grasped a math concept. He smiled at me often. Ordinarily, I was happy to stay late and talk to Mr. Edwards. But today...

"Ella, I wanted to give you these contest materials," said Mr. Edwards. He reached into his drawer and pulled out a brightly colored brochure: New York Math Olympics, it read in big gold letters. "The contest draws students from all over the city. Many are older than you are, but I think you will do very well. You should consider entering."

I looked at the brochure. "A math competition?"

"Yes," said Mr. Edwards. "It's very prestigious."

I was interested, even though I was itching to leave school and continue my quest for cash. Then I had a brainstorm.

"This contest—is there a prize?"

"Yes, there is," Mr. Edwards answered.

"Is it cash?" I asked eagerly.

Mr. Edwards looked at me strangely, as though I had just spoken to him in an alien language. Then he answered, "Well, no, but there is this lovely trophy." He pointed to the back page of the brochure with the photograph of three smiling children holding gold cups aloft.

"Oh," I said. "I see."

"Ella, is something wrong?"

"No. Why?"

"You seem distracted today. Maybe you're in a hurry?"

"Well, I do have a problem," I said. "In fact, I have a math problem."

"Really?"

"Yes. I need to turn $25 into $229 right away. So far, I don't have a good plan. But I think I know who can tell me the answer. That's why I'm kind of rushed."

Mr. Edwards smiled. "Well then, good luck."

"Thanks, Mr. Edwards."

I ran all the way home, but I was too late. When I burst through the door of my apartment, I saw the note on the refrigerator, held up by the big red ladybug magnet.

Hi, sweetie. I left for my business trip. I'll only be gone overnight. You be good for Dad. I left you money so you can go to the grocery store and buy dessert for you and Tom to eat tonight. I'll see you tomorrow. Love, Mom.

Rats! Mom had left already. I knew Mom's software company had raised lots of money to start its business. I had been planning to get tips from her on how to raise my own money. I was counting on Mom to tell me the secret to where money really grew.

But now, the plan was spoiled.

I called Madison.

"Too late, I missed her," I said to my friend when she picked up the phone.

"Well, didn't you say she'll be back tomorrow? That's not long," she said to me, typically looking on the bright side. But I was not in the mood.

"I can't wait till tomorrow," I said, stomping around the kitchen, cordless phone under my chin. "I can't wait another minute. I've been waiting all day. It's driving me crazy! I need a plan B."

"What's a plan B?" Madison wanted to know. "Is it a bug?"

"No, no, not 'bee' like honey, like the letter. Plan B is another strategy, a backup plan if your first plan of attack falls through. All smart business people have a plan B. My father talks about it all the time whenever he has a big case."

"Oh," said Madison. "So, what is your plan B?"

Just then, my brother Tom walked in. He was with his girlfriend, Samantha. The two giggled and looked all goofy with each other. They dropped their book bags by the door and came into the kitchen. Normally, I ignored them because they acted so weird together. But the sight of my brother gave me an idea.

"You know what, Madison? I think plan B just walked through the door. I'll call you back."

#

Half an hour later, I had been down to the grocery store and was back with a box of Mallomars, my brother's favorite cookie. I entered the apartment. The kitchen was empty. But there was only one backpack at the door, so Samantha must have left. I poured a glass of milk and took the cookies and went to my brother's room.

"Knock, knock," I said, because my hands were full and I couldn't knock for real.

"Go away," said Tom from behind the closed door.

I leaned close to the door so I was sure he could hear me. "I have Mallomars," I said into the keyhole.

In two seconds, the door sprang open. My brother can move fast for the right kind of cookies. "Wow, great, Mallomars! Hand 'em over." He reached for the box.

"Wait, I want to ask you something," I said.

"Ask me while I'm eating," he answered.

I smiled. That's exactly what I hoped he would say. I handed over the cookies and the milk and bounded into his room and jumped up on his bed. "I want to talk to you about money. I need to get some."

"Good luck," Tom said, his mouth full of cookie.

"I'm serious, Tom. I want to know how it's done. Do you have money?"

"Yes."

"How did you get it?"

"I got it for my Bar Mitzvah."

My heart sank at that. I would not have my Bat Mitzvah for another two years, so that was not going to be a quick way for me to raise money for my guitar. I was about to leave when Tom said something else that interested me.

"I got $250 in checks. But now it's up to $260." He reached into his desk drawer and pulled out a small blue book.

"What's that?"

"My bank book. After my Bar Mitzvah, Mom and Dad made me go down to Manhattan Bank and open an account. I put all my money in. Now it's up to $260."

"How did it grow?" I asked, picturing a grove of trees behind the Manhattan Bank building with money growing from their branches like leaves.

"Interest. When you put money in the bank, you earn interest. The bank uses your money to make investments or to give to others that need money loans. It pays you a little to do that. That's called interest."

"Weren't you afraid to leave your money there? What if they took it, loaned it to someone else, and didn't give it back?"

Tom swallowed a mouthful of cookies. "Dad explained to me that not anyone can just decide to open a bank. Banks are regulated by the government, and up to a relatively large amount—way more than I deposited—your money is insured. So, it's actually even safer than just carrying your money around in your wallet or even putting it in a piggy bank."

"So you earned $10 in interest?"

"Yes."

"In how long?"

"About a year. And actually, next year I am going to make a little more, $10.40, since now the interest payments that the bank is going to give me are going to be based not only on my initial deposit, but also on the interest that I've received."

I grabbed a piece of paper. This math was a little too hard for me to do in my head. At the rate Tom had described, which is 4 percent per year, it would take my $25 almost forever to grow enough to buy the guitar. Even if I combined babysitting with interest from a bank account, it still looked like a long, slow process. I was not getting any closer to my goal of being a middle school rock star.

"I don't think that's going to work for me," I said, flopping backward onto Tom's bed, my head hanging down over the side.

Upside down, Tom shook his head at me. "Nope, doesn't look like. Earning interest is a good strategy to make money, but only if you have a long-term plan and a large enough initial investment. Like me. I'm planning to use the money to finance a road trip with my friends when I go away to college. But that's a long way off. So I can afford to have my money grow over time."

"Well, I want something that will grow my money overnight," I said.

Tom laughed. "Sorry, I only know the slow way. You should ask Dad. Maybe he's got a tip for you. Thanks for the cookies."

I sat up. My answer was not here. I left Tom stuffing his face with Mallomars.

#

Just before dinner, the TV was on, and my dad was watching the business news. Normally I don't bother to listen, but tonight it seemed like a good resource for useful information. Maybe that's where they give out all the secrets to growing money? I sat down next to Dad to watch.

The reporter explained that something called the Federal Reserve made an announcement about interest rates, and that caused the S&P 500 stock index to go up by 1 percent.

"How long did it take stocks to go up one percent?" I asked Dad.

"That happened today," he said.

I thought about that. Tom was talking about a deposit that yielded a 4 percent return per year, and here there is something that can lead to a 1 percent gain in a day! That sounded much better.

"Dad," I said, "tell me about the stock market."

I asked so many questions at dinner that when Dad was finished with the dishes, he sat down at the table with me and a copy of the business section of the newspaper.

"Money grows in many ways," he said. "It can grow slowly, via interest, in a bank account. There are other ways money can grow, but they entail more risk than a bank account. For example, you can invest your money in the stock market."

"Is that like the supermarket?"

"Not really. The stock market is a system by which companies can raise money to grow and expand. They sell pieces of the company, called shares, to the public. You buy a share in the company, and that makes you a partial owner of the firm. Then, if the company is successful, it will positively affect the value of your stocks, or increase the value of your investment. If the company loses money, you may lose your investment.

"If you make good decisions in picking the right companies, with the right timing, you can make more money than you can by putting your money in the bank, but there is also a greater risk associated with it."

Dad opened up the newspaper and showed me where the stock prices were listed. The type was tiny, and there were lines and lines of company names and numbers. We looked together at the share prices. Then we went to the computer and looked up the stock history. He even showed me how to find information about a company that might help an investor decide whether or not buying the stock was a good idea.

"Dad, do you have money in the stock market?"

"Yes, your mother and I have investments. We have special accounts for you and your brother to help us save money for you to go to college. We also have an account that we plan to use to pay for our retirement."

"Can I make money in the stock market?"

"If you like, we can open an account and buy some shares, and we can follow them together and learn from how they perform."

"Will I make money right away?" I asked.

"I don't know. But probably not. Predicting the market is a very tough job. Researchers have shown that most people are not good stock movement predictors. Even most financial professionals have a hard time getting it right. But researchers found out that as long as you invest in a lot of different assets—that's called diversifying your portfolio—and you hold your investment for long time, more than ten years, you'll do better than if you just put your money in the bank."

I thought. But I kept listening in case there was a shortcut coming.

Dad went on. "Let's take an example from a company you like, Disney. I know you like their movies. The company saw its stock increase by one and a half percent today. But this was after the share decreased its value yesterday and the day before that. Anyone who purchased the shares three days ago has lost money. But, if you had purchased Walt Disney Company stock five years ago, for every dollar you invested then, you would now have $1.80. That's a better return than you would have gotten if you put your dollar in the bank.

"At the same time, there were other companies that saw their value drop dramatically in a very short time. You probably don't remember, but Uncle Max used to work as an engineer for a company called Enron in Texas. The managers of this company were involved in all kinds of bad behavior called fraud, and that caused the company to lose its money. When people found out about the fraud, the stock price dropped from around $90 to pennies, and investors that invested in their stocks, including Uncle Max, lost their investment.

"So, the stock market is fascinating, yet challenging, and hard to predict. But it's a great thing to learn. I'm very happy you want to learn about it."

I didn't have the heart to tell him that learning was fine and dandy, but what I really wanted was a way to turn my $25 into $229.

Finally, Dad said, "It's getting late, and you still need to do your homework."

I went back to my room. My head was spinning. There were many, many ways to make money, I learned. But so far, none of them would work for me.

chapter

THREE

The next day after school, I ran all the way home. I dropped my backpack in the hall, wrote a quick note to Mom, and then grabbed my guitar and headed for band practice.

In the movies and on TV, when you see kids start a band, you often see them practicing in a garage. But I live in Manhattan, so that's not really an option. There aren't that many garages here, and people who have them usually store tiny little expensive cars inside. It's not good band space.

But we're lucky because Madison's apartment building has a basement with a big storage room. It's a tight squeeze in the winter, but when spring arrives and everyone takes out their bikes and stuff, there's plenty of room for us. We'd been meeting there once a week to write and rehearse. Our goal was to compose enough great dance tunes to be chosen as the entertainment for our school's spring dance.

Madison lives two blocks from my house. By the time I got there, Madison and the guys were warming up. I strapped on my guitar and was all ready to get to work. But somehow, the rehearsal just never got into a groove.

Truth was, I was in a bad mood. I really wanted to be playing a new Daisy electric guitar. And instead, here I was, strumming my crummy old six-string. I felt like a loser. And I still had no idea how to get enough money to buy the guitar of my dreams. I tried to distract myself by focusing on the music. But that just seemed to make it worse. Every note we wrote sounded dull and boring, and the lyrics we were writing that afternoon didn't sound much better.

Empty pockets
All I got
Empty pockets
Not a lot
No dime, no nickel
My cash flow's more like a trickle
Bulls and bears
Stocks and deposits
They can't help me
In my life

"That doesn't rhyme," complained Jack, our bass player.

"Yeah. It doesn't really work," agreed Tyler.

"What about 'I can't compose it'? That rhymes," said Madison.

"The problem isn't the rhyme," said Tyler. "The problem is that the song is a bummer."

"Yeah," said Jack, "a huge bummer. Who would dance to that?"

My mood was not getting any better. "I'm doing the best I can with what I've got," I snapped. All my friends looked at me like I'd grown another head. I was just making the whole situation worse. I took my guitar strap off and sat down on the floor. "The truth is, I'm totally depressed today," I told them.

"How come?" asked Tyler.

Cute and sensitive. What a guy. I was almost too bummed to enjoy my crush. I sighed.

"I'm depressed because I really want a new guitar."

As usual, Madison tried to look on the bright side—even of my depression. "Lots of great songs are written by depressed people. You can use your bad mood to write a great song!"

"Yeah, but who will want to dance to 'The Great Bummer Song'?" asked Jack.

"He has a point," I told Madison. She shrugged.

"It's true. Nobody will want to dance to bummer songs. It's a problem," said Tyler. I sank even lower in my chair. "But for every problem, there is a solution," he added.

I sat up straight. Did Tyler know the secret to how to get money?

"You just need to go buy your new guitar," he said.

For a great guy, he could be pretty thick sometimes.

"It's not that easy," I told him. "I have $25 I need $204, plus tax, to buy the guitar."

"So ask your folks."

"Tried that."

"Tell them it's educational."

"Tried that, too."

"What did they say?"

"'Money doesn't grow on trees.'"

"Oh, I hate that," groaned Jack.

"Yeah, that's the worst," agreed Tyler.

"Almost as bad as 'We'll see,'" said Madison.

"Oh, and 'Wait until you're older.' That one just makes me want to scream," said Tyler.

I stood up. "Can we get back to the topic of my problem?" I asked.

Jack put his bass back on and began to pluck. "Actually, your problem isn't that hard to solve," he said.

"Really?" I brightened.

"Really," he said. "If you want money, you need to get a job."

He began to pick out a riff.

When you want money
When you want stuff
Don't ask your parents
Don't pray for luck

What you need
You need to succeed
Is a job
Get a job
Get a Job
Get a J-O-B
Because nothing you want is
Gonna grow on a tree
Get a job
Get a job
Get a job today
Because for what you want
You're gonna have to pay

We didn't write any great music that afternoon, but I left the rehearsal feeling better than when I'd arrived. I didn't have my guitar yet. But I did have a plan.

chapter

FOUR

The next day was Saturday, which was great because it meant I had all day to find a job. The morning was bright and sunny, and after I finished my chores, I met up with Madison in front of her apartment building. We walked together out onto Broadway, the biggest street near my house.

It wasn't quite noon, and already there were tons of people on the street. Dad always says: "You can get anything you want on lower Broadway." I was hoping he was right. I really wanted to get a job.

For luck, we went by the store to visit my Daisy guitar first. There she was in the window, just waiting for me. "Soon I'm going to come back and buy you," I said to my prize through the glass. Madison pumped her fists in the air in a silent cheer. Then we headed back to Broadway.

The first store we went to was Cheap Charlie's . They sell clothing that is so old, it's supposed to be cool, like leather jackets worn by real bikers and bowling shirts with names like Bubba and Morrie stitched into the fabric.

We went in, and I walked up to the counter with Madison.

"Hi, I'm Ella. I'm looking for a job."

The girl behind the counter was wearing a black T-shirt, ripped at the shoulder. Her hair was pink and gold and standing up straight like a shark fin. She had at least five earrings in the ear we could see. She was filing her fingernails. They were painted black.

She didn't even look at us. I tried again.

"Hello? I'm looking for a job. Do you have any openings?"

Still nothing. I looked at Madison and shrugged.

"Nice hair," Madison offered. That did the trick. The girl looked at us. I took my opening.

"Hi, I'm Ella. I'm looking—"

"No kids."

"What?"

"We don't sell kids' clothing."

"No, no. I don't want to buy anything."

"Then get out."

"Wait, no! What I mean is—"

"Frankie!" the girl yelled.

A huge man wearing army camouflage appeared. "Yeah?" he grunted.

The girl pointed to us and then jerked her thumb at the door.

"But we just want—" I started to say.

Next thing I knew, Madison and I were out on the street, squinting in the sun.

"And stay out," growled Frankie, stepping back inside and pulling the door shut behind him.

"No problem," I muttered.

We started to walk down the street. "No big deal," I said to Madison. "I wouldn't want to work there anyway."

"Yeah, that store didn't have a lot of positive energy," Madison agreed.

"Right," I said. "That was actually a lucky break."

But my luck didn't seem to turn into a job offer. The next clothing store we tried, The Nearly New, the man told me they didn't need any help. Ditto Sneaker City. The guy behind the counter at the Good Morning Deli was really nice and gave us both candy, but didn't seem to understand what I wanted. No matter what I said to him, he replied, "Have a nice day."

Back on Broadway, the sun was high in the sky and it was starting to get pretty warm. So when Madison spotted the Village Greenery, I followed her. I wasn't sure a flower shop was quite right for me, but it sure was nice and cool inside. The store was filled with buckets of flowers, pots full of tall, winding growing things, and in the center, there was a rock formation fishpond. We stood over it, looking at our reflections in the water, admiring the huge orange goldfish swimming under the foot-high waterfall. It looked like a nice cool way to spend a warm afternoon. But I had business to attend to.

I walked around the leafy store looking for a grown-up to ask about a job. "Hello? Hello?" I called.

"Hello," a voice finally returned. "How can I help you today?" The woman who emerged from behind all the plants was tall, wearing a green apron, and had white flowers twisted into her silver hair. She was smiling. I thought, So I took my chance.

"Hi, my name is Ella. I am looking for a job. I am trying to earn enough money to buy an electric guitar— really the guitar of my dreams. I know money doesn't grow on trees. But maybe it grows in a plant store. This is a really nice place, and I think your fish are super cool. Do you have any job openings?"

The woman smiled. "Hi, Ella. My name is Fern. I'm the owner of this store, so I'm especially glad you like my store and my fish."

"Fern?" I said. "Really?"

"Really," she said, smiling more broadly. "My husband said it was a sign that I was meant to be in the plant business."

"Once, when my class went to the botanical gardens, I saw a flower called the Ellamae Agapanthus. Maybe I'm meant to be in the plant business, too," I said hopefully.

"Maybe," said Fern. "But I'm afraid I can't offer you a job here."

"Why not?" I asked.

Fern walked back a bit and stood behind her counter. "I really couldn't hire a girl your age to work in the store. There are a lot of responsibilities to working in a store like this one. You need to have good customer service skills. You need to be able to work the cash register—"

"Oh, I'd be great at that. I'm top of my class in math," I told Fern. "I can even calculate sales tax," I added, remembering how my father explained to me that the cost of most products in New York City is often 8.375 percent more than what's printed on the price tag, because of the sales tax. I turned back to face the fishpond. "Quick, Madison, give me a number."

"Thirteen," said Madison, then quickly, "no, wait, nineteen. Thirteen is unlucky."

I glared at Madison for a second. This was no time for her superstitions! But then I quickly got back to my math problem. "New York sales tax is 8.375 percent. So if the price tag says $19, then the total cost would be $20.59, with sales tax."

I smiled proudly. I knew I was right.

Fern seemed impressed. "Well, you certainly are good at math."

"Thank you."

"And I'm sure you could work the cash register."

"Oh, yes!"

"If you could reach it."

I looked past Fern and saw that the top of her counter was pretty high—almost over my head. I could see the cash register was on top of it, but it was so high up, I couldn't see the numbers at all. In fact, when Fern demonstrated how the register works, the cash drawer popped out right at my eye level.

"Yikes!" yelped Madison, jumping back.

"Yes, sorry girls. This store is not set up for young workers. Also, there are laws in New York about hiring young people. For most jobs, you must at least be a teenager. Maybe in a few years."

I groaned. "A few years. I can't possibly wait that long. I need a way to earn money this year. Right now, even."

Fern looked sympathetic. "You could try babysitting."

I looked over at Madison and crossed my eyes.

"Or a lemonade stand."

Right as she said that, the image of a nice, tall, cool glass of lemonade popped into my head. What could be better on this warm spring day? Who wouldn't want one this second? Why, everyone walking down Broadway in the hot sun was probably thinking,

Madison was right beside me. "Are you thinking what I'm thinking?" I asked her.

"I think I'm thinking what you're thinking," she said. "I'm thinking I'm thirsty. And I'm probably not the only one."

"You got it, sister!" I turned to Fern. "Thanks anyway!"

"Good luck, girls," she called as we headed for the door.

I linked arms with Madison, and we ran out of the store, back onto Broadway. On the sidewalk in the sun, with the hot, thirsty people all around us, we hatched a plan.

"Quick," I said. "Let's get into the lemonade business before it gets cloudy or something."

And we ran for home.

chapter

FIVE

Madison and I ran back to my apartment and got my babysitting money—all $25 of it. Then we went straight to the supermarket. Lemons were cheap—69¢ each. But I didn't want to spend all day squeezing lemons.

"We should be outside selling as soon as possible. It's hot right now," I said.

Madison agreed. So we paid $5.99 for a big container of instant lemonade. We also bought cups ($3.49), a big Styrofoam cooler ($11.99), and a box of straws shaped like giraffes ($2.89).

"They're so cute!" Madison insisted. I thought they might be good for sales, so I agreed. The bill came to $24.36. We just made it.

Back in my apartment, we mixed up the lemonade in my mom's king-sized beach thermos.

"How much should we charge?" I asked Madison.

"How about fifty cents per cup?" she suggested. "Giraffe straws are free."

"Sounds good."

We made a sign that read "Lemonade: 50¢." And then we lugged everything back out to Broadway. But when we set up in front of the deli, the counter man who had been so nice to us in the morning came out waving his arms.

"Not here! Not here! Can't sell here!" he yelled, waving. "You can't sell in front of my place. Go sell in front of your place!"

"Okay, okay, don't have a cow," I muttered. Madison and I hauled everything back around the corner to my apartment building—on the shady side of Mercer Street.

"At least we won't get chased off," I said to Madison as we set up shop.

We'd no sooner set out our cups and sign when a mom and two kids walked by. "Ooooh, lemonade!" they yelled. "We want lemonade! We want lemonade!"

Madison and I smiled. The mom smiled back at us. "Three?" I asked our first customer.

"Um, no, these cups look pretty big. One will be fine," she answered.

I poured one cup, and Madison put in three giraffe straws. We were on our way.

For the next hour, we took turns walking up and down in front of the building yelling, "Lemonade! Fifty cents!" Most of the people coming in and out of my building stopped to buy a cup. Most of the people walking by on the street didn't. But I felt good; my pockets were getting heavy with our proceeds. I began to hum the songs I would soon play on my new guitar.

It was almost two o'clock when Mike Garcia, the super in my building, arrived for his afternoon shift.

"Hello, ladies," he greeted us as he approached the building.

"Hi, Mike. Want to buy a nice cool glass of lemonade? Only fifty cents," I said.

"Don't mind if I do," he answered, reaching into his pocket for money as Madison poured.

"Uh-oh," I heard Madison say. I turned to look at her. She almost never said that, so I knew something must be up.

"What's wrong?" I asked.

"We're all out. This is the last glass," she said, tipping the thermos so the last drops spilled out.

"All out? How can that be? We have all these cups left," I said, pointing to the stack. "And it's only two o'clock. We could sell all day!"

"Nope. We're all out," said Madison. "But we still have plenty of giraffe straws!"

I rolled my eyes.

"Well, since this is the last glass of the day, I am truly honored to receive it," said Mike, handing me a dollar bill. "You can keep the change," he said as he took his drink and headed toward the building.

Two o'clock and we were all out? That was disappointing. But we still had made a ton of money, I was sure. My pockets were bulging.

We sat down on the bench under the dogwood tree and began to count. It took a while, since it was mostly coins. And then we had the total: $18.50.

"That can't be right," I told Madison. "Let's count again."

We did. $18.50.

We had less money than when we started!

"Oh no," I groaned, putting my head in my hands.

"It's not so bad," said Madison, patting my shoulder.

"Yes, it is!" I shouted. "Of course it's bad! We didn't make enough money. We didn't make any money at all. In fact, we lost money!"

Madison shrugged. "Well, it could be worse," she said.

I didn't say anything. I wanted to cry, I was so upset.

"I think maybe I'll go home now," she said finally.

"Whatever," I answered. I was too bummed out to say anything else.

I sat on the bench after Madison left, looking at my cups full of quarters. How had this gone so wrong?

I gathered up all my stuff and lugged it up to my apartment. When I got there, my mom was at the kitchen table. Her laptop was open, and her papers were spread all around. I dropped my failed lemonade materials on the counter and sat down at the table beside her with a thud.

She looked at me. "Why so glum?" she asked.

So I told her the whole story. I told her about how I tried to get a job and no one would hire me. How I tried to sell lemonade and lost money. How I was never, ever going to get enough money to buy my beloved guitar.

"Selling things is a terrible way to make money," I declared.

My mom closed up her laptop and came over to give me a hug. Then she sat back down. "Actually, that's not true. Selling things is a good idea. You just have to do it the right way."

"What did I do wrong? It's a perfect day for lemonade," I said.

"Yes," she agreed. "Your environmental conditions are excellent. But what other factors did you consider?"

"What other ones are there?"

"Well, price compared to cost, for example."

"We charged fifty cents a cup."

"How did you arrive at that number?"

"I don't know. It sounded good at the time."

Mom laughed. "Well, you'd be better off learning beforehand what price the market will bear," she said.

"What does that mean?"

"That means it's wise to learn what your product is worth to consumers—and how much they are willing to pay for it. Also, you need to evaluate your cost to produce this item. Can you find ways to reduce the cost of production? If not, you may want to consider selling something else. You want to pick a product on which you will make a profit."

"A profit would be good."

"Yes."

"So how do I do that?"

"You need to do market research. Go to the stores; check out the prices they charge for items similar to yours. Pay attention to which drinks are the big sellers. That will help you price your own drinks."

I took one of Mom's scrap papers and began writing this down. In big letters at the top of the page I wrote: DO MARKET RESEARCH!

"What else?" I asked.

"Consider your costs," she said. "Maybe buying the cups at the supermarket isn't the best idea. I just saw that these cups cost half price at the liquidation store.

"Also, it looks like the cups you picked are a little big. You may want to consider buying smaller cups. The smaller cups are cheaper, so you can save there, plus they hold less lemonade. You may be able to sell the smaller cups for the same price that you were charging for the large cups. "And, honey, what are your production capabilities?"

"What's that?"

"How much lemonade can you make? Could you sell more if you had more prepared? What are your limits?

"Also, you may want to rethink these straws. I know they're cool," continued my mother. "But are they really needed? Maybe the answer for that is yes. Maybe

they attract customers. But maybe they're not neces-
sary, and given the tight profit margin you're facing,
you should reconsider them. Especially since it looks
like you didn't use very many of them.

"Finally, you need to consider your location," she
said. "You need a certain amount of potential customers to walk by in a certain amount of time so that it will
be worth your effort to set up shop here. Today, people who live in our building bought from you. But will
enough new customers walk by to make this a good
location? You may want to consider a different location
with a higher level of potential customer traffic."

"We tried Broadway, but the deli guy chased us
away."

Mom considered this. "I suggest you find a location that is high traffic—that means a lot of your potential customers will be there—and then make a deal
with the property owner."

"What kind of deal?"

"Maybe offer the owner a cut of your profits. Or
some other benefit the property owner might appreciate."

I didn't want to give away my profits. I was already
facing negative profits and had a hard time controlling
my costs. Paying someone money I already didn't have
enough of did not make much sense to me. So I made a
note on my list: THINK OF SOMETHING TO OFFER LOCA-
TION OWNER.

"And then?" I asked.

"You need to make a marketing plan."

"What's that?"

"A way to tell people what you are selling and encourage them to buy it."

"Like a sign?"

"That's a start."

Now my brain was starting up again. "Maybe flyers?"

"That's an idea. Be sure to consider the cost of the flyers in your planning. Paper, printing…"

I was starting to feel excited again. I began to sketch out a sign on some of Mom's scrap paper.

Just before dinner, I called Madison. I was relieved to find out she wasn't mad at me for being grouchy before.

"Don't make any plans for tomorrow," I told her. "I figured out what went wrong in our lemonade stand today."

"Really?" she asked.

"Really," I said. "And tomorrow, we're going to do it again. This time, the right way."

"Sounds great!" she answered. And for once, I was happy about her positive attitude.

That night, I lay in bed, looking at the ceiling, trying to think up a new location, one with lots of thirsty kids…

Just as I was falling asleep, it came to me: the downtown rec center!

I closed my eyes and fell asleep, dreaming of lemonade pitchers pouring out dollar bills, so many of them, they filled up the storage room in Madison's basement, up to the windows, out onto the street, and ran like a river down Broadway.

chapter

SIX

The sun woke me up on Sunday morning. Normally, I don't like waking up all squinty with the sun in my eyes, but just this one time, I was happy. It was a sunny day. A perfect day for selling lemonade! I bounced out of bed.

After breakfast, I met Madison in front of her building.

"What's all that?" she asked, pointing at my armload of school supplies. I had notebooks, clipboards, pens, pencils, and a super-sized eraser shaped like a sneaker.

"Research materials," I told her. "We made a big mistake yesterday by rushing into our business without doing proper market research. This time, we're going to be smart about it."

I held out the clipboard. Madison didn't take it.

"What's the matter?" I asked. "Are you mad at me about yesterday? I'm sorry I was such a jerk about it."

"No, I'm not mad," she said.

"Well, what then?"

Madison hesitated. Then she blurted out, "We thought we were going to grow you money, and we didn't. We shrank it! I feel terrible. I feel so bad, I think maybe you should take the money you still have and just put it somewhere safe. Somewhere where it can't shrink anymore."

I thought about that a minute. It was nice that she was worried about me. She was the sweetest best friend a girl could have. But I knew enough about business by now to understand that she had it all wrong.

"Sure, it hurts when things don't go well right at the start. But that's no reason to quit and never try again," I told her. "My mother says lots of successful businesspeople try a lot of times before they make money. But it's never a good business plan to just stop trying. If you put your money away and never try to do anything with it, how can it grow?"

By the time I finished my speech, Madison was smiling. "Okay," she said. "I'm game if you are."

"Totally," I said. I handed her a clipboard.

"Okay, so like I said, our problem yesterday was that we rushed into business without doing any market research."

"What's that?"

"That's when you study the kinds of products already for sale that are like your product. You learn about what products are popular, what are not, and how people like to buy them."

"So we need to study lemonade?"

"We need to study things kids drink."

"Just kids? Didn't grown-ups buy our lemonade yesterday?"

"You have a point," I replied, "but I was talking to my mom yesterday, and she said lots of products are successful because they have a target audience—a group of people who are really into the product. And I think our target is kids, even though we did pick up a few grown-ups here and there."

"Okay," said Madison. "Where should we start? The coffee shop? They sell drinks there."

"Well, our product is targeted for those who want to drink while walking, so a coffee shop or restaurant wouldn't be quite right. Let's start with the supermarket," I said.

With our clipboards in hand, we walked into the Metro Market. There are lots of supermarkets in our neighborhood, but the Metro Market is every kid's favorite. That's because the owner, Mrs. Milano, is a really nice lady and never yells at kids who come into her store. And also because she has two really big orange tabby cats, named Sugar and Spice, who patrol the store and keep the mice away. They're nice cats and always purr when you pet them.

As soon as we walked in, I noticed the big display at the front of the store: Cool Ice Energy Blast. The clear plastic bottles held liquid blue like the sky, and they were stacked almost to the ceiling. And that was just the beginning. After the Cool Ice display came a long aisle of nothing but drinks of all kinds, some on the shelf, others chilling in the cooler. I pulled out my clipboard and started to make notes.

"Hello, girls. Need help finding anything?" It was Mrs. Milano.

"Hi, Mrs. Milano," said Madison. "No thanks. We're not here to buy anything right now. We're doing research."

"For a school project?"

Madison looked at me.

"Well…it's educational," I offered. I wasn't sure how—or if—to tell Mrs. Milano that I hoped to be her next competitor in the beverage business. But lucky for me, I didn't have to face that particular problem.

"Okay, girls. Have fun," said Mrs. Milano as she walked back into her office behind the cash registers.

Madison and I breathed a sigh of relief and got back to work.

We were in the Metro Market for more than an hour. And boy, did we learn a lot of important things. I made notes on my clipboard:

There are lots of drinks for sale: milk, soda, water, fruit juice.

Drinks come in lots of sizes, from one pint to one liter.

Most drinks cost more than one dollar. Many cost more than two dollars.

Kids reached for drinks that came in funny colors.

Lots of people didn't even bother to look at all the drinks in the store. They just grabbed a bottle from the Cool Ice display while they were standing in line at the cash register.

"What's next?" asked Madison.

"We need to decide which products in this store are our competition," I said.

Madison and I decided our lemonade was in competition with the fruit-based drinks. We looked at their prices, and we were very happy: Most were way more than a dollar. Some were even three dollars and more.

"Looks like we can charge more than we were thinking yesterday," I said.

"Great, are we ready to sell again?"

"No, not yet. We still have more research to do."

First, Madison and I went to the playground and surveyed the moms: how much would you pay for a cup of lemonade?

"What's the point if we don't have lemonade to sell right now?" asked Madison as we made the rounds of the moms on the park benches.

"We're trying to see if the customer is price sensitive," I explained. "My mom told me about it the other day. Before you set your own price, you need to know what price will bring in the most customers at the most profit to us."

With our survey results in hand, we went back to my apartment for lunch. My mom made us peanut butter and jelly sandwiches. She looked over my clipboard as we munched.

"Not bad," she said. "Very interesting information. But so far, you just have information from moms. What about kids your age? What will they pay?"

Madison groaned. "Do we have to go back out to the same playground?"

"No," said Mom. "There are lots of ways to do market research. In person is one way. And another…"

I looked at where she was pointing: the phone.

"Don't tie it up all day," she warned us as she left the kitchen.

After lunch, Madison and I took turns dialing the kids in our class. Most were happy to be part of the survey. Some even put their brothers and sisters on the phone to give their opinions.

We were about halfway down the class list and in a groove. Madison was reading off the phone numbers and recording the answers. I had my market research pitch all smooth and confident-sounding. I felt like a TV news anchor.

"Okay, who's this one?" I asked Madison after I'd dialed the number and heard it start to ring.

"Tyler."

"Tyler!" I yelped, jumping down off the kitchen stool where I'd been sitting, dropping the phone to the floor just as I heard his voice.

"Hello? Hello?"

I picked up the phone and stood frozen with it in my hand.

"Hello, Tyler?" prompted Madison.

"I can't call Tyler on the phone," I said.

"You just did."

"Hello? Ella? Is that you?"

I put my hand over the receiver and hissed to Madison, "I've never called Tyler! We always make band rehearsal arrangements at school. What if he thinks this means I like him? What if he thinks I'm calling to ask him out?"

"You do like him."

"Madison!"

"And he's on the phone now, so you have to do something before he hangs up and thinks you pranked him."

Yikes! That would be bad. I put the phone to my ear.

"Uh, hi, Tyler. It's Ella."

"I know," he said. "Hi."

I tried to get my brain to function, but I was a blank.

"How are you?" I managed.

"Fine," he said.

This was a nightmare.

Madison held up her clipboard and pointed to it. I took a deep breath and started talking.

"Hi, Tyler. I'm calling because I'm doing market research for a new business I'm starting. Do you have time to answer a few short questions about your beverage preferences?"

"Sure," he said. "What do you want to know?"

I went through our ten questions, smooth and professional, repeating all the answers back so that Madison could record them on her clipboard. Tyler's voice sounded great on the phone. Even his voice was cute!

We completed the survey, and Madison flipped the page on her pad. That was my cue to say thanks and good-bye.

Instead I said, "Question eleven."

Madison looked at me and raised her eyebrows.

"What do you prefer to do on the weekends? Play sports, watch TV, go to the movies."

"Movies," said Tyler.

"Question twelve."

Madison held up her hands in a "What are you doing?" gesture. I ignored her.

"What is your favorite kind of fast food: pizza, tacos, hot dogs?"

"Pizza. With a side of garlic knots."

"Question thirteen."

Madison smacked her forehead with the palm of her hand and rolled her eyes.

"What is your favorite color?"

"Blue," said Tyler. "Are these questions still about what I like to drink?"

Busted! But I thought fast.

"Sort of. They're the get-to-know-the-customer questions," I said.

"Oh," said Tyler. There was a long pause. "What's favorite color?" he asked.

"Red," I told him.

"Favorite food?"

"Pizza."

"Favorite activity on the weekends?"

"Movies, I guess. Also music."

"Me, too," said Tyler. "I guess I don't have to ask you your favorite flower. It's the daisy."

It took me a minute to realize what he was talking about. "Oh, yeah, my guitar."

"Right," he said.

We both said nothing. And finally Tyler said, "Well, okay. Bye."

"Bye," I said.

I hung up the phone and turned back to Madison. She had her arms folded like she might be mad, but she was smiling.

"So, if you're ready to get back to …"

"That was business."

"Since when are we in the movie-slash-pizza-slash-favorite color business?"

"Well, the information might come in handy," I said.

"It sure would," agreed Madison. "Especially if you were to call Tyler up and ask him to go out on a date."

"Madison!"

"Which you should."

"Omigosh."

"Why not?"

"I couldn't do that."

"You practically just did," said Madison.

"That was different."

"What."

I shrugged her off. But even as we got back to work, I couldn't shake the feeling of Tyler's voice in my brain.

By early afternoon, we'd done the full class list, and I thought we had enough information to go on.

"Now, we need to scout a location. And I have the perfect spot in mind."

We walked east, past the dress shops and the pizza restaurant and my favorite music store, until we got to the river and my destination: The Lower Manhattan Recreational Center. The center was really a whole bunch of places. It was a big indoor gym and also a series of playgrounds and playing fields. As we walked up, we could see little kids on the swings and Little League players out on the baseball diamonds.

We also saw a bunch of older kids lining up to take turns on the new section of the skateboard park. I recognized it as we got closer—Tom had been talking about it for weeks. The sign in the park called it The Wave, but the kids all called it The Death Wish. It was so popular, the line snaked all the way along the fence, halfway to the entrance. Tons of kids were standing there, waiting, all hot and sweaty. No Cool Ice Energy Drink display in sight.

"This is it!" I said to Madison. "This is our location! They're mostly older kids, so they'll probably have money on them. And they're hot from skating and bored standing in line. It's perfect."

I looked around. Vendors selling everything from ice cream to homemade empanadas worked the edge of the park. They all had one thing in common: wheels. Whether it was a car or a bicycle or, in the case of the empanada man, a shopping cart, all the vendors rolled along.

"Looks to me like it's okay so long as you can keep moving," I said.

"I have an idea for how we can do that!" Madison said.

We hiked back to her apartment, and Madison disappeared into her mother's huge coat closet. She emerged a few minutes later, covered in scarves and hats, pulling a little red wagon. "It was Evan's, back when he was little," she said. "But now that he has Rollerblades, he never uses it."

"Cool!" I said.

We hauled the wagon to my house and loaded it up: the thermos and the shoebox that now held my money—mostly in quarters. We went to the Metro Market and purchased another box of lemonade mix, a package of a hundred small cups, and some food coloring. We had already invested in a big Styrofoam cooler, so our cost for supplies was lower this time. Mrs. Milano didn't seem to mind that we paid for it all in coins.

When we got to the rec center, we mixed up the lemonade using water from the drinking fountain. Then I squeezed in blue and red food coloring. "Kids will pay more for a drink if it looks good," I said. "Remember all those kids buying that blue drink from the Metro Market…"

Then we pulled the red wagon slowly along the Death Wish line.

"Purple lemonade!" I yelled. "Fresh purple lemonade for sale! Get some while it lasts!"

"Purple?" said one kid on the line. I recognized him—Zachary, from Tom's class at school.

"You bet," I answered.

"Purple as a boysenberry!" Madison chimed in.

I didn't know what that was, but Zachary seemed okay with it. "How much?" he asked.

"One dollar," I answered.

Zach reached into his cargo pants and pulled out a crumpled dollar bill. I poured the purple lemonade into a clear plastic cup. He downed the whole thing in two gulps, smacked his lips, and got back in the line. Moments later, he was at the top of the ridge of The Death Wish. His lips were stained purple. He came barreling down the incline, leaping at the end into a full 360 and landing, wheels on the ground, fists in the air.

Kids all over the skate park cheered.

"Woo hoo!"

"Yeah, Zach!"

"You rock, man!"

Zachary got in the line again, and when he reached our location, he dug out another dollar and said, "Give me another shot of the purple stuff. Did you see my last move? It's like rocket fuel."

Madison poured Zachary another cup. He drank it down, and this time he not only did a 360, but added a two-hand touch hop at the end that was straight out of the X Games. The skate park went nuts. After two cups of our lemonade, Zachary's whole mouth was ringed in purple and his white teeth gleamed when he smiled.

"Yeah, baby!" he shouted, pumping his fists in the air. "I'm the Purple Rage!"

Pretty soon, all the guys were lining up for a shot of purple lemonade before hitting The Death Wish. Zachary had stopped skating and was now walking around the park, recounting the tale of his two fabulous runs, flashing his purple lips/white teeth smile.

An hour later, the thermos was empty. I ran to the water fountain to remix. We were out of red, so I mixed the last of the blue with yellow.

"Green lemonade!" I announced as I pulled the wagon back past the skate park fence.

"Fork over your green for some green!" yelled Madison.

"Hey, that's a great slogan," I told her.

"Thanks," she answered. "Maybe we can turn it into a song when you get your guitar and our band takes off."

The rest of the afternoon sped by. The skateboarders all bought lemonade. Some bought two cups. We used up all our drink mix, cups, and food coloring. Finally, I sat down to count our money.

This time we were selling the lemonade in a smaller cup, so we sold more at a higher price.

Sixty-six cups at $1 per cup was $66.

$66!

Even after subtracting the cost of our supplies, $18, we still had $48. From one day! That, combined with the $18.50 I already had, gave me $66.50.

"Can you do orange?" asked Danny Parker, one of the other cool skateboard kids, as we packed up.

"We sure can," I told him. "Come back again. And tell your friends."

That night, Madison stayed for dinner, and we sat around the dinner table and told my parents about our great day in the cool-colored lemonade business.

"See what you can do when you first understand your market?" said Mom. "You took the time to research what you were selling and the price you were selling it for, and that paid off for you. Plus, you made a smart decision to set up in a location with teens. They're less price sensitive than moms."

"What's that supposed to mean?" Tom grumbled.

"It means you care more about being cool than you do about saving money," Mom said to him.

"Whatever," Tom answered.

Mom served everyone seconds of macaroni and cheese.

"The question now is, how will you build on your success?" she said.

"Do the same thing tomorrow?" Madison ventured.

"Yes, but now you are not a new business. You are a going concern, so you need to be aware of managing your customer base while also searching for growth opportunities. How will you get your customers to come back?"

"We promised them orange."

"Good. Now, what about new customers? How will you attract them?"

Madison and I looked at each other and shrugged.

Mom kept talking. "Well, think for a minute. What worked for you today?"

"Zachary. He drank the first cup and then spent the rest of the afternoon telling everyone in the park how great it was."

Mom smiled. "That's called word-of-mouth advertising. And it's very effective. People are much more willing to try something when a friend recommends it. And Zachary is not just anyone. He's what they call an influencer."

"What is that?"

"That's someone that other people look to for ideas about fashion or entertainment. Or about what the new, cool drink is," Mom said. "He other people's choices. So the question is: what can you do to convince Zachary to talk about your product some more? Or even better, get his friends to talk about it."

"Maybe if we offered him free drinks for life?" Madison said.

"Or gave him a discount," I tried.

"Never happen," said Tom.

"Shut up," I said.

"No, wait, Ella. Let's hear what Tom has to say. Tom, why do you say Zachary won't want to be a booster for cool-colored lemonade tomorrow?" asked Mom.

"Because it's old news. Because he did it today and it was cool, and now it's done. A cool guy won't go running back to do it all over again just for a free drink. That doesn't make him seem cool at all," Tom said.

I thought about this. "So, to talk about our drink some more, it would need to be cool for Zachary," I said.

"Right," said Tom.

I thought about it while we cleared the table and brought out the cookies for dessert. Tom was eating those Mallomars again. I remembered when I was little, I liked a cookie called Elegants. But that was because my name is Ella and I thought they named the cookie after me. I made Mom buy them every week.

I was munching Mallomars, and then I had my brainstorm. "We'll name a drink after him!"

I looked at Mom. She was smiling and nodding. I was already planning the next day's activities.

chapter

SEVEN

"Ella! Come into the kitchen and clean up this mess, please!"

I was not quite ready for school, but my mom had that "Right now!" voice, so I hurried down the hall, hopping and pulling my socks on as I went.

"Coming, Mom!" I yelled.

"And what is all this paper all over the kitchen table?" my mom said as I got to the kitchen.

"Market research. Sorry, Mom. I'll get that all cleaned up," I said, starting to grab up all the cups I'd left around the kitchen.

"Ella! What is your music doing in my CD player?" It was Tom, yelling from his room. He did not sound happy. I'm only allowed to use his CD player if I promise to put it back exactly the way I found it—which, obviously, I had forgotten to do.

"Sorry, Tom. Just trying to learn some new songs for the band," I yelled, shoving an armful of cups into the trash and moving quickly to the mess I'd left on the kitchen table. As I moved through the room, I glanced at the clock: 7:51 a.m. I thought.

"Well, get your stuff out of my room, or I'll put a lock on the door," said Tom, now in the kitchen, pouring himself some cereal and leaning up against the dishwasher to eat. It looked good, but I didn't have time for Corn Flakes.

"Okay, okay, don't have a cow," I said to him.

"You're supposed to leave my stuff exactly like you found it, which does not include leaving your stupid music in my CD player."

"My music isn't stupid!"

"Ella, the table, please. So the family can eat," Mom said.

"Right."

"Why are we out of toner?" It was my dad, yelling from the living room. "And paper. We are out of paper. Did someone print out a hundred pages of something?"

"I did. Flyers for my lemonade business," I said. I'd stopped calling it a lemonade stand. I thought "business" sounded more official.

Dad came into the kitchen. He was carrying one of his computer disks from work and holding the empty ink cartridge from the computer. He started to say something. Then he stopped.

"This place is a mess," he said.

"I know. I'm cleaning up," I said, sweeping the last of the cups from the counter and turning to the table. There really was a lot of paper spread around, I had to admit. And the clock was now reading 7:59. Almost time to leave for school.

"Dad, can you tell her to quit screwing up all my technology!"

"Ella, don't use all the paper."

"Dad!"

"And respect your brother's technology," he added.

"Fine, whatever," I muttered.

"Ella, the kitchen table is a common area, so you can't use it to store your belongings," Mom was saying.

"Okay, okay, I'll just take it all and stuff it into Tom's CD player," I said.

"Mom!"

"Ella, respecting your brother's space is not something you can take lightly."

The intercom buzzed. It was Madison. She was in the lobby. No surprise since we meet every day in my lobby at the same time to walk to school. This was the first time in a year I hadn't been waiting for her downstairs.

"Can you tell her I'm coming in a minute?" I called to my dad, standing near the intercom box. I swept everything I could carry off the table and ran into my room and dumped the papers on my bed. I was about to run back out when I realized my homework had been on my bed—and was now under the paperwork pile. I began to dig.

"Ella! You'll be late for school!" It was Mom.

Found the homework! I stuffed it into my backpack and ran back to the kitchen, which was still pretty messy. I took another armload of paper and a Pop-Tart from the counter—it would have to do for breakfast.

The buzzer rang again.

"What about my CD player?"

"What about this mess?"

Bzzzzz, bzzzzz, bzzzzzzz, rang the buzzer.

"What about everybody just get off my back!" I yelled, spraying Pop-Tart crumbs out of my mouth. I didn't even care. "I've got a lot to do here, and I'm doing my best, so if everybody could just stuff a sock in it, I would really appreciate it!"

Everyone was silent for a moment. Then the intercom buzzed again.

"I'm coming!" I yelled. Which was kind of funny, since Madison was ten floors down in the lobby and couldn't hear me. But I didn't feel like laughing, even at my own joke.

Dad stepped up. "Why don't we tell Madison to walk ahead, and I'll take you to school this morning?" he said.

"Fine," I answered.

For the next five minutes, Dad helped me clean up the cups and papers and put them away in my room. Then he showed me how to add paper to the printer and change the toner cartridge so that the next person could use the printer. Finally, he dug his old portable

CD player out of the front closet and promised to buy some new batteries for it.

"That way, you can prep for your band without bothering your brother," he said.

"Okay," I said. "Thanks."

Mom and Tom went back to their morning routine, but Dad sat down on one of the kitchen stools and patted the one next to him for me to have a seat.

"Okay, now that we've solved the immediate crisis, let's talk about this. What's going on with you, Squeaky?"

Usually, I hate it when he uses my baby nickname like that. But right at that moment, I didn't mind so much.

"There's so much to do," I told him. "There's so much to keep track of, and I can't keep it all straight. I didn't think it would make my brain hurt like this." I picked up a copy of one of my mom's business magazines from the kitchen counter. On the cover, a man in a yellow T-shirt with an @ symbol on his chest was smiling. "Look at him. He's in business. He's not stressed out. He's not going crazy. He's smiling. What's wrong with me?"

I put my head in my hands on the table. Dad patted my shoulder.

"Well, first of all, he has more experience than you do in business. So he's a little better at managing his time than the average sixth-grader," he said.

"It takes experience to pick up cups and change the toner?"

"Everything takes experience," he said. "One of the things you learn as you gain experience is that running a business is not just about doing everything yourself. It's about delegating—leading others to contribute to the business, too."

"That sounds better than what I've been doing," I said.

"But another thing to keep in mind: This man does not go around picking up anything, except maybe at his own house. He's not an entrepreneur. He's an investor," Dad said. "Remember you asked me the other day about stocks?"

"Oh, right, the way you buy partial ownership of a company," I said.

"Yes. Well, stocks are just one way an investor can make money. There are other financial instruments that one can invest in, such as bonds. In a bond, the government or a particular corporation borrows money from investors. A bond is a kind of contract, and it can be short-term or long-term, and as with anything else in finance, there is risk associated with return. The higher the potential risk, the higher the potential return.

"Professional investors often use many financial products," Dad went on, "some of them very sophisticated, and their prices depend on other financial assets. These are called derivatives. Maybe if you want to this summer, we can invest together. We can research some stocks, buy some shares, look at some bonds, and track their performance. It can be our summer project."

That sounded good to me. I love a good summer project. One year, we built a model of the White House out of Popsicle sticks, and another we tracked pictures from the Hubble telescope. But just when I was starting to feel good about it, I had a thought.

"But Dad, the summer is still a month away. I can't wait a month to make money."

He laughed. "Ella, even when we start this project in the summer, you won't get your money right away. A smart investor takes a long view—as many as ten years—to collect a profit. But it's worth it in the long run. You will have the money to spend when you go to college."

College? My heart sank. That was forever from now. "I was hoping for something a little faster," I said.

"I know," Dad answered. "And I think you're on the right track with your lemonade stand. You just need to learn to manage your time so that you're not trying to do all things at once. For example, you might want to watch less television so that you have time to get your work done."

No TV? Crazy talk! On the other hand, if it could help me get my guitar...

"I'll think it over," I told him.

"Good. Now let's get you to school."

Dad hailed a taxi outside of our apartment, so I wasn't even late for school, which was a relief because I have a perfect on-time record, and I didn't want to break it this late in the school year. I got to the front doors right as Alice, the lady who runs the office, was starting to pull them closed.

"Just made it, young lady," she said to me as I scooted by. I smiled at her and ran up to my class.

I felt better, but my buzz did not last. Right after third period, when we were on our way to science, I caught up with Jack and Tyler in the hall and reminded them that we had band rehearsal after school.

"Don't be late," I told them.

"I can't come," said Jack. "I have baseball this afternoon. We're in the playoffs."

"Can't you miss it?" I asked him.

"No," he said.

"Why not?" I asked.

"Well, because it's the playoffs and my team is counting on me," he said. "And because I don't want to miss it. I want to play."

I swung my backpack over my shoulder so hard it flew up in the air, and Madison had to duck to avoid getting clobbered.

"Well, that's just great! I'm putting everything I have into this band, and so is Madison, and you just blow it off for a baseball game!" I fumed.

"I'm not blowing off the band," argued Jack. "Just this one rehearsal."

"Same thing!"

"It is not!"

"Is too!"

"Is not!"

"Is too!"

"Both of you just cool it," said Tyler. He turned to me. "Maybe we could rehearse tomorrow?"

"Busy," I said. "Busy running a business to make enough money to buy a new guitar that will make this band a sensation because I care. Unlike some people."

"Whatever!" said Jack.

"Yeah, whatever to you, too," I shot back. It wasn't a very good comeback, but I dropped all my books when I said it, so the crash helped make my point.

Madison and Jack moved along the hall to go to science. Tyler helped me pick up my books.

"Are you going to the school dance tonight?" he asked.

"Whatever," I said again. I was too mad to be nice. Even though Tyler looked really cute right at that moment, and I could tell he was trying to be friendly, I was just not in the mood.

I stewed about it all day: how much work I was doing, how much I wanted to succeed, and how hard it was to get my friends on board even though it seemed really clear what we had to do for all of us to be famous. By the time I got home, I didn't really feel mad anymore. I just felt like a jerk for yelling at my friends. And I felt stupid for passing up the chance to talk to Tyler about going to the dance. I put our band CD on the player my dad gave me, but even with the music playing, I couldn't shake my mood.

At 5:00 p.m., my mom came into my room. "Aren't you going to get ready for the dance?" she asked.

"I don't think I'm going. I'm not sure my friends are talking to me."

I told her the story of what happened right before third-period science.

Mom listened. Then she said, "Well, the best thing you can do is say you are sorry and make it up to them. Leadership is not just about knowing what to do. It's about being able to work with people so that they want to follow your lead."

I decided she was right. I got up and got dressed, and Dad walked me to the dance at the school gym. I saw Madison right away. She seemed happy to see me, so I guessed she wasn't too mad. Then I saw Jack and Tyler and went up to them. They were holding cups of punch and listening to the music playing over the school PA system.

"Lame band," I said to them, pouring myself some punch.

They shrugged. Tyler smiled a little.

"Listen, I'm sorry I was just a jerk before," I said to Jack.

"A total jerk," he corrected.

"Yeah," I said. "That's what I meant. A total jerk. Sorry about that."

"Well, okay."

"Okay."

We sipped a little more punch.

"How was the game?" I asked him.

"We won, seven to five," Jack said.

"Great, congratulations," I said.

Jack gulped the rest of his punch. "I can maybe rehearse tomorrow," he said.

"I'm selling lemonade," I reminded him.

"Okay. Maybe I can help with that," he said.

I remembered what Dad said about letting people help and not trying to do everything myself. "That'd be good," I said. "We'll be at the skateboard park at noon."

"Okay, then. See you tomorrow," he said, and he walked off.

Tyler and I stood alone by the punch bowl.

"Want to dance?" Tyler asked

"Sure," I said.

We moved out to the dance floor, where a ton of other sixth-graders were already twisting and turning.

"Do I need to apologize to you, too?" I asked him as we started dancing.

"No," he said. "I don't mind when you get all worked up like that."

"You don't?"

"No," he said. "I kind of like it. It's exciting. Like fireworks."

"Oh," I said, wondering if it was a good thing to be like fireworks. Tyler was smiling, so I guessed so.

"You're right," he said, finally. "This is a lame band."

"We're better," I said.

"Way better," he agreed. "And just wait till you get your new guitar!"

chapter

EIGHT

After the dance, I came home and got ready for bed right away. I wanted to get a good night's sleep so that I'd be ready for the big sales day in the morning. I changed into pajamas, brushed my teeth, said good night to Mom, Dad, and Tom, who were all in the living room still watching the pirate movie Dad had rented, and I crawled into bed.

But my plans for a restful night did not go as I hoped. Even though I was snug in my bed, I could not get comfortable. I tossed and turned. I turned the light on. I turned the light off. I opened the shade. I closed the shade. I turned on the fan. I turned off the fan. Still,

I could not get to sleep. I kept thinking about Saturday and the lemonade stand and how many things could go wrong: In the next room, I could hear the faint sounds of the pirate movie—cannons and sword fights and battle cries. I wondered if pirate kings lay awake at night before a big attack, worrying over the details.

It was dark and quiet in the apartment when I finally fell asleep. But even then it wasn't very restful.

I dreamed it was Saturday and we were all at the skate park, setting up. The weather was fine, the sun was shining. I rolled up in the wagon with all our supplies and Madison, Tyler, and Jack were there waiting for me.

As we got ready, a crowd of kids began to form. They were all hot and thirsty and chatting about how great it would be to drink lemonade. They formed a line that stretched from the skate park, all the way down the river, to the big glass office towers at the tip of Manhattan Island. I was already counting my money in my head. It was going to be a great day.

I mixed up the first pitcher of lemonade and dyed it neon green. Then I poured a glass and handed it to Tyler. "On the house," I said.

He gave me a big smile in return. He tilted his head back and took a long, slow gulp of the ice-cold bright green lemonade.

Then he spat it out on the ground.

"Yuck!" he yelled, loud enough for the whole line of kids to hear. "Disgusting!" And he made a face that looked like the dragon lizard at the zoo.

"Huh? What are you talking about?" I asked him, my voice sounding far away, like I was deep in a cave.

Tyler just walked away. I turned to Madison. She had poured herself a cup and taken a swallow. Now she was making the same dragon lizard face.

"Salty," she said, and her voice sounded like she was standing inside my brain, shouting. "Ella, you bought salt instead of sugar!"

I looked at the line of kids. Instead of laughing and talking, now they were grumbling and complaining. Some of them had begun to chant, "Lemonade now! Lemonade now!"

"Okay, okay!" I yelled to the crowd. "Just take it easy! I'm doing the best I can. Be patient. And be quiet!"

"Ella, are you okay, honey?" It was Mom.

I looked around. I wasn't in the park, trying to sell a pitcher of salty lemonade to a crowd of thirsty, angry kids. Instead, I was sitting up in my bed. My mom had turned on the light and sat down next to me.

"Are you all right? Did you have a nightmare?"

I nodded.

"Do you want to talk about it?"

"I dreamed I put salt instead of sugar into the lemonade and a whole mob of kids was about to pound me," I told her.

She smiled and put her arm around me. "I know just how you feel. I always worry before a big day at the office. Once, before a big presentation, I dreamed I went into the conference room, but the presentation wouldn't boot up, and all the clients around the table took off their shoes and threw them at me."

I had to laugh at that.

She hugged me. "It's okay to be nervous. A little nervous energy is good for business. It makes you try harder and be more focused. Just don't let it get the best of you," she said. "Remember that this is business: Even if everything goes wrong, there's always another day. As long as you don't give up, you haven't lost."

I hugged her back. "Okay. I'll try to keep that in mind."

I lay down, and she turned off the light. Finally, I fell asleep.

When I woke up, the first thing I noticed was the sun streaming through my window. It was going to be a nice hot day. Hooray!

Instead of running around like a maniac like I'd done before, this time, I was more organized in my preparation. First, I made a list of what I would need to accomplish for the day. I called Madison and gave her some chores to do. "I'm delegating these to you," I told her. "That means I'm spreading the work around so we'll all be ready to open for business this afternoon."

"Got it, Chief," she responded.

I gathered up the materials I needed from home. Later I met Madison at the Metro Market with our seed money to shop for supplies. Now that we were experienced shoppers, the trip was quick. We picked up more cups and lemonade ingredients and food coloring. Within ten minutes, we were at the checkout line.

"Nice day for a lemonade stand," said Mrs. Milano as we paid for our stuff. "Good luck, girls."

"Thanks, Mrs. Milano," I said as we gathered up our materials.

After lunch, we loaded up the wagon and headed for the skate park. The sun was high in the sky. The park was filled with kids. We rolled up to our usual spot. I gave Madison the stack of flyers to hand out around the playground and the nearby ball fields. And I began to set up.

It wasn't easy. I had to lug the water, mix the drinks, set up the cups, and try not to spill anything. I didn't want to waste any of our materials, since that would cut into our profit. I hummed a guitar riff to myself to keep focused on my goal. Last, I taped my big sign, "Rainbow Lemonade! $1 per cup!", to the mop I'd borrowed from my mother's cleaning closet, and I wedged it into the axle of the wagon. It stuck straight up in the air, just like I hoped.

"Higher than the Golden Arches." It was Tyler. He and Jack walked over to where we had set up shop.

"Hi, guys," I said to them.

"Can we help?" asked Tyler.

"Yeah," said Jack. "For the good of the band," he added.

"Sure," I said. Madison had just come back from handing out the flyers. I gave her the rest of the cups to set up and turned to the boys. "You can be our guerilla marketing team."

"Gorillas!" huffed Jack.

Tyler raised his eyebrows at me.

"No, no, it's not what you think," I said. Guys could be so touchy! I reached into my back pocket and pulled out a folded-up magazine article I'd torn from Dad's business magazine. It was all about guerilla marketing. "This is the kind of marketing that you don't have to pay a ton of money for," I explained. "Lots of small businesses use it to get attention. Instead of paying for television commercials or putting your ad on the side of a bus, you come up with something interesting, something attention-getting, something free, that gets consumers interested in your product."

"Like what?" Tyler wanted to know.

"Well, like this guy in the article. He wanted people to come to his chiropractor business, so he set up a chair in the park and gave free back massages and discount coupons," I said. "Then, this other woman wanted to be an investment advisor. So she printed up a T-shirt that said 'Ask me how to get rich,' and she walked around the shopping mall in it. Lots of people asked her, and she was able to get lots of new customers."

"So do we need T-shirts?" Jack asked.

"No, we don't," said Tyler. "We just need to do something that will make people look at us and think 'lemonade.'"

"Exactly!" Tyler was so cute when he was smart. "So you want to come up with something that hypes the benefits of our drink," I said. "You know, that it's cool, and close by, and not salty."

"Not salty?" Madison said. "What's that about?"

"Never mind," I said, shaking off my nightmare. I turned back to the boys. "You guys are good at getting attention. I'm sure you'll come up with something great," I added, trying to use my best "delegation" voice.

Mom said it should be strong without being bossy. It was not easy to do, since I can be very bossy sometimes.

But the guys seemed to be okay with their direction. They went off to the side of the bike path to brainstorm.

We had pitchers at the ready and all the cups lined up when we heard it start. Tyler and Jack had set up on one of the hills in the middle of the park. They had two turned-over plastic pails, and Tyler was pounding out a hip-hop beat. Jack stood in front, doing his best robot, and began to rap.

> *So here's the rap*
> *It's where it's at*
> *Telling all the facts*
> *About rainbow lemonade*
> *'Cause we're the guys*
> *With the supplies*
> *Won't tell you lies*
> *About rainbow lemonade*
> *It's the coolest juice*
> *That's on the loose*
> *And that's the truth*
> *About rainbow lemonade*
> *So buy a cup*
> *And drink it up*
> *'Cause it's wassup*
> *It's rainbow lemonade*

A crowd of kids had started to gather. With the drum beat still going, Jack broke his rap and made the announcement, "Go buy yourself a cup of rainbow lemonade. It's on sale now. And then come back and join our rap. The best rainbow lemonade rap of the afternoon wins a prize."

"What's the prize?" one kid wanted to know.

Jack looked around. Tyler called out, "Jack will give you the shirt off his back!"

Jack looked surprised a moment. And then he smiled and waved to the crowd. They cheered, and a group broke away to line up at our wagon.

Our first batch, ruby red, sold out in thirty minutes. Meanwhile, two other kids had picked up containers and joined Tyler's drum corps. The air was filled with rapping and clapping. We were on our second set of pitchers and I was looking for the blue food coloring when Cliff, the Parks Department employee who was in charge of the skate park, came by.

"I was over by the band shell when I heard the drums. Where can I get this rainbow lemonade?" he asked, smiling because he knew the answer.

I offered him a free glass. He paid anyway.

"You guys are doing great. I should hire you to sell raffle tickets for the playground renovation. You are obviously naturals," he said, sipping his lemonade and bopping a little, in a funny, grown-up way, to the drumbeat. "Well, see you around. Don't forget to clean up when you're all done today."

"Don't worry, we won't," I promised him.

"Have a nice day," Madison added. She was really getting into the whole customer service thing.

Cliff raised his cup in response and walked away.

By 5:00 p.m., the lemonade was gone, Tyler had polled the crowd, and the winning rapper—a girl named Denise—was wearing Jack's T-shirt, and my dad had turned up to see how we were doing.

"Great," said Madison.

"I think," I said. "I haven't counted the money yet."

"Well, better do that before you do anything else."

So I delegated the cleanup chores and started to count. By the time the guys had carried the cups to the trash and Madison had washed out the pitcher and picked up any stray flyers, I had the news: we took in $62—a $46 profit!

"Wow," I said.

"Woo hoo!" yelled Madison.

"We rock," said Tyler, giving Jack a high five.

My dad looked almost as happy as we were. "I'm very impressed," he said. "Ella, I think your team deserves a reward. How about we go for ice cream? My treat."

More cheers. We headed across the street to Sweet Dreams, the best candy and ice cream shop in Manhattan. Dad handed Jack his sweatshirt since he'd donated his own shirt to the rap contest. We got a booth in the back. Madison ordered her usual—strawberry. Jack ordered a flavor called Jawbreaker—blue with pieces of hard candy stuck in.

"I'll have a mint chocolate chip, please," I said when it was my turn.

"Me, too," said Tyler.

I looked across at him.

"It's my favorite," he added.

"Me, too," I said.

But even as we ate our reward, I was starting to feel bummed out. Sure, we sold a lot of lemonade. And sure, it was fun. And we worked as a team. But $112.50 was a long way from what I needed to buy the guitar. And the last day of school was fast approaching.

"Why so glum, Squeaky?" my dad wanted to know.

"Dad, at this rate, I won't have my new guitar before school's out for summer. We'll never have the chance to be the coolest band in the sixth grade."

"Can't you be the coolest band in the seventh grade?" Dad asked.

Madison shook her head. "Too much competition."

"Yeah," said Tyler. "We pretty much need to establish our rep now."

"Otherwise, it could take us years," said Jack.

I slumped in my seat. "This is such a bummer. We started a successful lemonade business, but it won't get us to our goal in time. What a waste."

I put my head down on the table.

"No, wait," said Madison. "We can't give up. There must be something else we can do."

"There isn't," I said.

"Are you sure?" Dad said.

I picked my head up. "Like what? Something else we could sell?"

"Like candy?" said Jack

"Or ice cream?" said Tyler.

Dad sipped his iced tea. "Products are one thing you could sell. But it's not the only thing. In addition to goods, like ice cream and lemonade, businesses can sell services."

"What's that?" I asked.

"A service is something you do for someone in exchange for money. You don't sell a product—you sell your skill, your ability, your expertise."

"Like Mom sells her software design?"

"Yes, exactly. Mom doesn't sell the disks or the computers. She sells the technical skills it takes to make them run. She's paid not for a product, but for a service."

"What kind of services could we sell? What kinds are there?" Tyler wanted to know.

"There are lots of different kinds of services," Dad answered. "Advice, creative work, technology know-how, entertainment—"

At that I sat up straight. Entertainment! Of course!

I looked at Madison. She was sitting up straight just like me. I knew she was thinking the same thing I was thinking. So we said it at the same time: "A concert!"

The guys looked at us like we were crazy. Even Dad.

I explained. "Cliff from the Parks Department already came by to tell us how great we were and how he should have hired us to sell raffle tickets for the new playground equipment. So let's do it. We'll do a concert in the band shell with half the money going to the playground fund and half to the electric guitar fund."

"Can we even do a concert if you don't have your electric guitar?" asked Tyler.

"Sure," I said. "Maybe it won't be the best we could ever play, but we can play. You guys were great today, and you only had plastic buckets turned upside down. In fact, we should bring up the winner of the contest today to perform her rap. Can you remember who she was?"

"Yeah," said Tyler. "Her name was Denise."

"She shouldn't be too hard to spot. She's wearing my shirt," Jack added.

"Let's go find Cliff and see what he thinks of our idea," I said.

We all left the ice cream shop and headed back toward the park. The guitar of my dreams was closer than ever.

chapter

NINE

That night after dinner, I helped Tom clean up the kitchen as fast as I could so I could start planning our concert. Our meeting with Cliff had gone super well. He liked the idea of a concert, and he was willing to split the box office (that's money from ticket sales, I learned) with us. I was sitting on my bed working up a song list in the back of my math notebook when Mom and Dad surprised me by coming into my room and sitting down on the edge of my bed.

For a second, I was nervous. Sitting-on-the-bed conversations are sometimes a sign that I'm in trouble. But then I saw they were both smiling.

"Ella, we are both very impressed with the effort you're making to raise money for your guitar," Mom said.

"Thanks!" I answered, wondering where this conversation was going.

"And we're particularly happy with the way you've researched important business concepts," said Dad. "That's really using your brain."

Now I knew something good was coming. Mom and Dad always love it when I use my brain. This was a good sign.

"So, we've got a proposition for you," Dad continued. "It involves a new business concept that you may not have considered."

I was confused. I thought I was using all the concepts they'd taught me. But I sat up straight and listened.

"We want to make you a business loan," Dad said.

"What's that?"

"In a business loan, a person, a company with money, or a bank lends a certain amount of money to a businessperson—often someone like you who is starting or expanding a business. The two parties make a deal. They decide on the amount of the loan and also the terms," said Dad.

"Terms?"

"That's what the businessperson agrees to pay back. Usually, the full amount plus interest," said Mom.

"Interest like Tom's Bar Mitzvah money is earning in the bank?"

"Exactly," Mom said. "They also agree when the money will be repaid. It might be in one lump sum or over time."

"Now, we are willing to loan you the amount you need to buy your electric guitar," began Dad.

"Yippee!" I interrupted.

Mom put her hands up. "Wait a minute," she said, "because we have some conditions."

I sat back to hear them.

"First," said Mom, "we want to see your marketing plans for the concert."

"Sure, I can show you the signs we're using."

"Signs are a good start. But remember, if you want people to come and pay money to hear you play, you need to let them know about the concert and give them a reason to pick your event over anything else they might want to do that day," Mom said. "A marketing plan is more than signs."

"Okay," I said.

"Also, you need to present your marketing plan to Cliff and get his okay, since he is your partner," she added.

"Mmmm," I answered, turning over my song list to make notes.

Dad jumped in again. "We'd like to see you do some research that shows us why this guitar is the best one for you and why you think this store is the best place to buy it. Have you looked at other stores? Considered their prices? Have you researched warranties? These are all factors when making a large purchase, and we want to see that you have considered all the important elements of this one."

I scribbled furiously to keep up.

"And finally, we decided that if we are happy with the preparations you are making, we will not charge you interest on the loan."

At least that was positive.

Next to the note I was scribbling, I began to do the math.

"Okay, so if $116.50 is the amount you're lending me and I have to pay you, then the concert needs to take in $233 so I can give half to you and half to Cliff."

Dad looked at my work. "You might want to consider cutting in the rest of the band on some of the money, since they're working hard, too, and ultimately you get to keep the guitar. Plus," he continued, "you will need to plan for expenses. You need a certain amount for expenses you know you will face, and then some more for expenses that may come up and surprise you."

My paper was filling up, so I got a clean sheet.

"Okay, I need $116.50 to pay off the amount of the guitar loan, at least $20 for each of the band members for a total of $60, and if that's the half for me and the band, then Cliff needs to get $176.50. On top of that we need $30 to cover marketing and show expenses and $20 for unexpected events, and that means the total amount I need to come up with—"

"Revenues," said Dad, reminding me of the word.

"Right. My total revenues need to be $403."

Mom and Dad stood up. "We'll leave you to work out a plan. When you're ready, you can show it to us, and we'll review it. If it's good, we'll make you the loan," said Mom.

As soon as they left, I called Madison, and we made plans to meet the next day after school with the boys to work out our plan. I was so close to getting my guitar!

chapter

TEN

"Why don't we try skywriting! Everyone would know about our concert!"

We were in Madison's basement, but there was no time for rehearsal today. We were busy brainstorming ideas for marketing our concert. I really wanted us to come up with something good in time for us to show to Cliff—and for me to be home for dinner by six. We only had a week to promote this concert. I wanted to get my guitar as soon as possible.

"Jack, we can't afford skywriting," said Tyler.

"Why not? How expensive can a lot of white smoke be?"

"Very, when you factor in the cost of the airplane!" I said.

"Oh. Good point," said Jack.

"But still, very creative idea, Jack," added Madison.

Everyone was being very reasonable and nice and supportive. But so far, we hadn't come up with anything good. I was starting to worry. If I couldn't get my guitar soon, there's no way we'd be ready to play at the concert on Sunday.

"Right now, what we need are ideas that are good, but cheap," I said, trying to keep everyone focused. "We don't have money for marketing, but that's okay. We can use the kind of marketing we used in the skate park to sell lemonade."

"Singing?" asked Tyler.

"No, no, I mean viral marketing. Remember how we sold a lot of lemonade by getting the cool kids to try it and then talk about it?"

Tyler thought for a moment. "So what we really need to do is come up with something that the cool kids will want to come to—and bring their friends," he said.

"Right."

"The more friends, the better," said Jack.

"Why don't we give a prize to the person who brings the most friends?" said Madison.

"What kind of prize?" I asked.

"Yeah, what kind of prize could we give that doesn't cost any money? Since we don't have any," said Jack.

"I was thinking about a song," said Madison.

I wasn't too sure about this. "I don't know, Madison. Doesn't everyone who comes to the concert get songs?"

"A special song. Just for that group of friends."

"That is totally cool," I agreed. "But it would be kind of hard to write a song on the spot like that."

"But we could write the frame of the song in advance," said Tyler. "Set up the lyrics, and just fill in the names at the last minute."

"Yes, that's it!" said Madison. "It's the friendship concert. Bring your friends; leave with your own original theme song. It's awesome!"

I had to agree; it did sound awesome.

And even better, the next day at school we found lots of kids thought so, too. During second-period independent reading, I circulated a survey of my class, to see how they would feel about the concert, the ticket price, and the prize. The prize got everyone's attention. And by yard time at lunch, they were all crowding around us.

"Do little sisters count?" Emory Harris wanted to know.

"Yes," I told her. "If she'll come to the concert with you, she counts. Little sisters are people, too," I added. After all, as a little sister myself, I felt like I should stick up for us.

"Will you sing it right there at the concert?" asked Cory Pike.

"Yes, we will take the names of the winning group, write the song during the intermission, and give its first live performance," said Tyler.

"Wow," said Justin Barnett. "Just wow. Your own song."

"I'm going to ask all my friends," said Serena Lee. "And maybe I'll make some new ones, just to be on the safe side."

After school, I left the other band members behind to put up signs and answer other questions. I ran home to finish my loan application.

First, I called Cliff at his office at the rec center and told him our marketing plan.

"Sounds great," he said. "Maybe I can get all my friends to come. Can I enter the contest?"

"Well, no, sorry. Only audience members. But we'll write a song for you anyway. *Cliff, you're just terriff, you lucky stiff…*"

"Just catch a whiff!" sang Cliff into the phone.

"Um, yeah, we'll work on that," I promised him. I hung up and got back to the rest of my application process.

It was almost five when Tom came into my room and found me on my computer.

"Whatcha doing, Squeaky?" he asked.

"Don't call me that. Finishing my loan application."

"Oh yeah, I heard about that. What do you have so far?" he asked, leaning over my shoulder to look at the screen.

I called up the file. I had a list of local music stores and their prices on the Daisy. I highlighted the price on Underground Sound to show it was at the low end of the range. I had a list of features that the Daisy had and how they would help the band and my music career.

"Good idea, adding the career stuff," Tom said. "Mom and Dad will like that. But just say 'music.' Don't bring up 'rock star.'"

I had all the information about the warranty. And finally, I downloaded two audio clips: one of an acoustic guitar playing "Happy Birthday," and another playing the same song on an electric guitar.

"Looks pretty good," Tom said. "The audio is super cool."

I smiled. Tom never said anything nice about me unless he really meant it.

"How are you going to get it to Mom and Dad?" he wanted to know.

"Print it out, I guess," I said.

"Yeah, but then you can't use your audio clips."

"Oh yeah, you're right. Bummer."

Tom thought a minute. "Wait here," he said, and disappeared for a minute. Then he came back—with the laptop he'd rebuilt with Dad last summer. "It'll look great in PowerPoint," he said. "Like a million bucks!"

"Or just $116.50," I said.

#

After dinner, Tom surprised me by volunteering to do all the dish chores—clearing the table and loading the dishwasher. I was shocked.

"Good luck, Ella," he whispered as he carried the plates to the sink.

Mom and Dad were still at the table, so I brought the laptop into the dining room and began the presentation.

I started with the clip of the acoustic guitar. Then I moved into the informational slides. After listing the benefits of the Daisy, both to me and the band, I pulled up the page for Underground Sound and clicked on the warranty page.

"You can see that this protects the buyer, provided the item is used correctly and according to the directions. So no skydiving," I added.

Mom and Dad laughed.

Next, I pulled up the Web page for the skate park band shell.

"The auditorium seats three hundred. We conducted a survey in Mrs. Hilary's second-period independent reading class and found more than eighty percent of our sample would be willing to pay two dollars to attend this concert. So we have set our ticket price at two dollars and are committed to selling two hundred tickets to cover the loan, payment to the band, and Cliff's fund for improvements to the skate park. Finally," I said, "here is our marketing plan."

I brought up a slide of our signs and then another with our Friends Forever Theme Song contest. In it, I had the song outline Tyler had composed; it was so cool. All we'd have to do on show day is fill in the blanks with the winning names.

I closed with the audio clip of the electric guitar.

Mom and Dad were quiet a moment. So quiet, even Tom poked his head around the corner from the kitchen to find out what was going on.

"What happened?" he mouthed to me.

I shrugged. I wondered for a second if I'd blown it. Maybe they didn't think I'd made a strong enough case for the guitar?

Then, Dad stood up, walked over to me, and shook my hand. "Congratulations," he said. "That was a very compelling presentation you made. We will loan you the money for the guitar. We can go together after school tomorrow to get it."

Mom stood up and gave me a hug. Even Tom gave a high five. I was so excited. I couldn't wait to call Madison. My electric guitar dream was coming true!

chapter

ELEVEN

After school, I spotted Dad right away as I came out of the building and into the yard.

"Ready?" he asked.

"Am I ever!" I told him.

Kids were swirling all around us as we made our way to the gates. I was trying to stay close to Dad and still dodge the backpacks. But when I shifted left, I ended up with a block to the back.

"Ooof!" I yelled.

"Sorry, Ella."

It was Tyler.

"Hi, Mr. Levy," Tyler said.

"Hello, Tyler."

We pushed along in the crowd for a few more paces with Tyler's backpack bumping my shoulder. When we made it to the sidewalk, I turned to Tyler and spoke quickly, before I lost my nerve.

"We're going to buy my Daisy. Want to come?"

"Wow, sure," said Tyler. "Today's the big day!"

I nodded. Suddenly I felt my brain going blank again. Why did that always happen when I was alone in a conversation with him? We walked along Eighth Street, toward the East Village, and all I could think of was: Finally, we arrived at Underground Sound. The owner, Zeb, met us at the door.

"So, Ella, it's the big day!"

"Hi, Zeb. It sure is."

"And I see you brought a date."

I dropped my head down in the hopes that no one would see me blush. When I stole a look over at Tyler, I saw he had his head down too. But he was smiling.

"This is Tyler," I told Zeb. "Best drummer below Fourteenth Street."

"Well, then, let's get this party started," said Zeb. He disappeared into the back room, and when he came back, he was holding Daisy. She was all strung and ready to play. Zeb had even added on a new shoulder strap and handed me a guitar pick that glimmered pink and purple, just like Daisy.

He draped the strap over my shoulder and bent down to plug in the amp. "How about a test drive?" he said.

For a minute I just stood there, with Daisy in my hands. She was beautiful. She made me feel beautiful. Everything seemed to fade away but Daisy and me.

Then Zeb's voice brought me back. "All set, downtown drummer boy?" he called.

I turned around. Zeb had set Tyler up behind a fully loaded five-piece drum kit—black with silver trim. I thought he looked older, somehow, up there on the platform with his sticks poised, ready to go.

"Take her in, drummer boy," called Zeb.

And Tyler began to play, rolling from a solo intro into a steady rock beat. I let it pound into me a minute. And then I came in.

At first, I riffed a few oldies favorites I'd learned in guitar class. All the grown-ups in the store started to clap. Then I moved into some of the music we'd written together in Madison's basement. And soon, Tyler and I were both singing.

Keep your dreams in your heart
Make your dreams where you start
Every day, every way
That's the love that will lead you
Keep your dreams on your mind
Make your dreams what you'll find
In your day, in your night
That's the love that will feed you

We finished, and I waited for Tyler to come down off the platform so we could take a bow together.

"Awesome!" he said as he grabbed my hand and we bowed.

"And the Grammy goes to…" said Zeb as he took Daisy from me to wrap her up for the trip home. As he prepared her case, Dad and I did our paperwork on the glass countertop. I signed the loan agreement. Zeb's assistant, Patti, was our witness. And finally, we all walked out of the store, and I was carrying Daisy.

"Congratulations," said Tyler. "You sound great on Daisy."

"Thanks. You sound great on that drum kit."

"Maybe I'll save up for it. You can give me tips on how to raise the money."

"Sure," I said.

We came to his building. "Okay, this is my stop. See you tomorrow," he said.

He stood there a moment, like he had something else to say but couldn't remember it. Was his mind doing that go-blank thing, too?

Eventually, he just turned and sprinted for his front door.

Dad and I headed for home.

"A great day," Dad said.

"Awesome," I answered.

chapter

TWELVE

The day of the concert arrived. I was nervous, and my stomach felt like it was hosting a butterfly slam-dance contest. But Mom insisted I eat lunch anyway.

"A good performance takes fuel," she said, putting a peanut butter and jelly sandwich down on the counter. "You need your energy for the crowd."

"I hope there's going to be a crowd," I answered, trying to stop biting my nails, instead nibbling on the sandwich. "What if nobody shows up?"

"I don't think that will happen," Mom said. "You've been promoting all week."

"That's true," I said.

"And you've been getting lots of feedback from kids at school who say they are coming."

"Yes, but what if something else came up today? Something better? I wish we'd spent more time looking at the calendar, figuring out the best date. What if this is a bad day? And all the kids who said they were coming today changed their minds and went someplace else?"

"All of them?"

"It could happen!" I insisted, my mouth full of sandwich.

Mom sat down at the counter next to me. "Ella, I know how you feel. You've got a lot riding on the concert today, and you've put a lot of time and effort into the event. I feel the same way on the day my company launches a product I've worked on," she said.

"You do?" I tried to picture my mom, sitting on her hands, trying not to bite her nails.

"Absolutely," she said. "The trick is to remember that you've done everything you can to make the day great, and now, you have to believe in your preparation and forge ahead. Give the day your best, and don't spend any time worrying about what you could have done differently. Today is the day to go for it. Showtime."

While she'd been talking, I realized I'd eaten my sandwich. Now I gulped down my apple juice, stood up, and said, "It's showtime!"

"You bet it is," Mom said, and she gave me a hug.

I met the band and Cliff at the skate park at three for one final rehearsal and setup. It didn't take as long as I thought it would, and soon Cliff went out front to set up the box office table and we all sat down on the stage and tried not to show how nervous we were.

"The Daisy sounds great," said Tyler.

"Thanks," I said. "I just hope enough people come so that I can pay off my loan."

"They will," said Madison. "I'm sure of it."

"How do you know?" asked Jack.

"I believe in our band," said Madison.

"Well, me too," said Jack, "but now we need to have a boatload of people believe too," he said gesturing at all the seats we'd set up.

Suddenly, it looked like a lot of seats. I wondered if we should fold some up and keep them to the side. I sat on my hands to keep from biting my nails again.

"What if nobody comes?" Jack continued.

"What if something better is going on today?" I said.

"What if something good is on television?" said Tyler.

"Yeah, that could be a problem," Jack said.

"Okay, okay, enough of that," Madison said firmly. "We're all going to have to chill, or we will freak out before the show. No negative energy allowed. Now, all of you, sit down on the stage, close your eyes and repeat after me: oooooom,.."

We all sat down, like she said.

"Why are we saying oooooom?" asked Tyler.

Madison answered him without opening her eyes. "Because it helps drown out the negative thoughts in your head. And we've got plenty of those, so let's start oooooom-ing. Oooooom. Oooooom."

We all sat on the stage and did as she said. And I have to admit, after a few times, all I could hear was "oooooom," and all the what-ifs had drifted out of my head. We were really getting into an oooooom grove when I heard one more thing: Cliff's voice shouting.

"Hey! Where are you guys?" he yelled.

I jumped up and popped out from behind the curtain. Cliff was standing in the center aisle, amid a sea of empty chairs.

"What's up, Cliff?" I asked him. The butterflies in my stomach had started up again. A million possibilities ran through my head at once: The show was cancelled. We were ruined. My Daisy was going back to the store. But then Cliff came closer to the stage, and I could see he was smiling.

"There's a huge crowd outside," he said. "You're going to need more chairs."

All four of us ran to the window, and of course, Cliff was right. A major mob of kids was already milling around outside, starting to form a sloppy line to the door. They were clumped together in groups. Some of the groups—girls, mostly—were dressed alike, the same color shirt or hair bands. The guys mostly stood around in packs and punched each other in the shoulder a lot.

"Wow," said Tyler.

"Yeah, awesome," agreed Jack. "Look at all the kids who came out."

"And brought their friends," said Madison.

"Yes," I said, putting my arm around Madison's shoulder. "It's good to have friends."

We had fifteen minutes till the doors opened. We scurried around, setting up chairs. Then, our parents arrived, and they helped out. At four forty-five, we went backstage to get ready, and Cliff went out front to open the box office. From behind the curtain, we could hear the kids coming in, calling to each other, getting seats, scraping their chairs on the floor.

Cliff came backstage right before curtain. "I haven't counted it all yet, but the box office take looks great so far. Have a great show!"

Finally, we went out onstage, and the curtain went up. I couldn't believe how many kids were there.

"Must be the whole sixth grade," said Madison.

"And part of the seventh!" said Jack.

"Well, let's give them what they came for," I said. I revved up the Daisy. The crowd cheered, and we started to play.

We gave our best performance ever. The audience was clapping and singing the whole time and even dancing in the aisles. Even the parents in the back looked like they were having a good time. At intermission, Cliff passed us the friends lists he'd collected at the box office—and we had a tie! Carlos Acevedo and Ariella Wilson both had eleven friends on their lists.

"What do we do?" I wondered.

"Only one thing to do," said Tyler, scribbling the names furiously on the notebook he'd brought and stashed backstage. "Sing the song twice."

So we did. And the crowd went wild. We had to play two encores before Cliff came onstage and announced that the concert was over. "But I'm sure you'll all join me in hoping the band will be back for more performances this summer," he said.

Everyone clapped and cheered as we took one last bow. I wished the moment would last forever.

That night, we went to Tony's Pizza to celebrate. 232 kids had paid to see us! We'd counted all the money with Cliff after the show and given him his share first: $232 for the rec center, $96 for the other band members, and $116.50 for my parents to pay off the Daisy. She was all mine now. I just knew we were going to do great things together. This was just the beginning. I even had $19.50 left after paying off all my debts. I sprang for some orders of garlic knots.

Still, sitting in the booth at Tony's, I felt kind of weird. Even though I'd eaten two slices of pizza, I felt a little empty.

"Why so glum, Ella?" my dad wanted to know.

"I'm not sure," I told him. "I feel kind of sad about… something."

Mom came over and joined us. "It's post-launch letdown," she said. "After the big day, the rush passes, and then you have to go back to normal."

"But I don't want to go back to normal," I said. "Growing Daisy was the most exciting thing I've ever done. Even when it was hard. Even when it seemed like it wasn't going to work. I don't want to stop feeling like that."

"Well then," Dad said, "it sounds like you need a new challenge."

"Like what?"

"I don't know," Dad said. "But I expect you'll know it when you see it."

I pondered this a moment. I tried Madison's mind-clearing trick: I closed my eyes and whispered, "Oooooom, oooooom," to push all the negative thoughts out of my head. Then I opened my eyes and looked around. Standing at the other end of the restaurant was Tyler. He smiled at me. That's when I had the idea.

I got up and walked over to him. "So, Tyler, I had this idea," I started.

"Okay," he answered.

"Since the one song we wrote for the audience today went over so well, I was thinking we should expand the effort."

"You mean write more songs?"

"Yes, write more songs. Some for us to sing. Others for us to sell to other people."

"Yeah, like if a guy wanted to ask a girl out, he could hire us to write him a song," said Tyler.

"Yes," I said. "What do you think?"

"It's a great idea," he said.

"So we'll work together this summer," I said.

"You bet," he answered.

And then I took a deep breath and went for it.

"And maybe we could go to the movies sometime. Like on a date," I said.

I looked at him. He was still smiling.

"Sure," he said. "Sounds good."

It was going to be a great summer.

—The End—

About the Authors

Orly Sade is a Ph.D in finance-business administration and a professor of finance at the business schools of New York University and The Hebrew University of Jerusalem. She also teaches graduate students at IE (Madrid) and NES (Moscow). She created the story of Ella and her entrepreneurial quest using accurate financial and economics concepts. Ellen Neuborne is an award-winning writer and a former editor at Business-Week Magazine.

Made in the USA
Monee, IL
21 February 2022